Endorsements

"Wafa Shami writes a beautiful orchard story of devotion, labor, and harvesting in which nothing terrible happens. Palestinians deserve more days in which nothing terrible happens. Here is life, shining, ripe and succulent, singing of culture, history, tradition and the dinner table too."

Naomi Shihab Nye

"This story, primarily intended for children, can be enjoyed by people of all ages. The principles of community, family, country and love are beautifully shared through the elements of the olives, oil and warm maklouba. This is the story of Palestine. Shami takes us on a virtual tour of a typical day in the life of a family in a Palestinian town, told through the eyes of children."

Hussam Ayloush

"Wafa Shami's story about the annual olive harvest is a wonderful outing for children young and old alike to learn about Palestinian culture, family life and connection to their land and heritage. This story about the fruits of the land and their labor reflects the safe and joyful time the harvest should be for all. Shami's story also serves as a beautiful invitation for people from around the world to visit Palestine, stand in solidarity with the people during the harvest, and help secure their land and traditions for future generations of Palestinians."

Estee Chandler

"Nearly 55% of Palestinians are children. We tend to forget that. Shami's lovely children stories like this one on olive harvest remind us and reconnect us (kids and grown-ups) to each other and to the land in a heart-warming way."

Mazin Qumsiyeh

"A beautiful portrayal of the most important harvest in Palestine. You have skillfully opened the reader's imagination to exactly what the olive tree means to Palestinians: a connection to the land, food, family, livelihood and most important community. Your readers may very well be the first generation of Palestinians to witness the olive trees blossom in peace in a free Palestine. Thank you for contributing toward this path."

ISBN: 978-0-9600147-1-2
0-9600147-1-3

Illustrations by Shaima' Farouki
September 2019
Production by: Gate Advertising
www.gateadv.net
+972-569878101

Printed in the United States of America
U.S. $9.99

An Arabic version of this story is available on amazon.

To my father who loved planting trees.

May he Rest in Peace

Special thanks to the late Jad and Julia Mogannam,
quoted in this story, who gave me this life experience.

May they Rest in Peace.

It's a warm fall Thursday in the town of Ramallah, Palestine, about six miles from the big city of Jerusalem.

Noor and Manal live next door to each other, and they're having a quiet afternoon hanging out, playing and chatting.

Manal's dad approaches the girls and asks if they would like to go for a ride.

Noor and Manal excitedly jump into the car. As they head out on a winding country road, the girls begin noticing all the olive groves whizzing by. And they squeal with delight when Manal's dad reminds them that tomorrow is the first day of the olive harvest. Noor and Manal make a game of trying to count the endless number of olive trees covering the gentle hills on both sides of the road.

Manal's dad says that the land of Palestine is known worldwide for its olive trees, but that few people understand the magic of these sacred and ancient beings.

"Did you know that it takes up to five years for an olive tree to start producing olives? Did you know that these trees are older than I am? In fact, most of the trees you see along this road are hundreds of years old!"

Noor is surprised to hear all this.

"How an olive tree can last for so many years?" she wants to know.

Manal's dad replies, "That is their nature.
An olive tree is tough and resilient; its thick roots are entwined deep into the land, just like the Palestinian people."The girls are tickled to hear this, and they erupt in laughter.

It has become a tradition: every fall, Noor enjoys harvesting with her friend and neighbor Manal, whose family owns several olive tree groves. It's a fun activity for the entire community. And it's important, too, because so many Palestinian farmers rely on the olive trees to make their living.

Noor and Manal and their families and friends will gather tomorrow to help pick the olives. The girls can barely contain their excitement.

Here comes Friday. It's dawn, and the sky is purple. Noor's mom wakes her up so she can get ready to join the harvest.

Although Noor is still sleepy and groggy, she jumps out of bed filled with excitement about this great day. Noor quickly washes her face and brushes her teeth as she throws on her clothes, then she rushes next door to Manal's house.

Manal greets Noor at the front door exclaiming, "I'm so glad you're here! My dad is already getting the car ready -- he wants to leave right NOW. My mom will join us later."

It's a crisp morning. As the girls arrive at the olive grove, the sun is rising over the hilltops.

There are already several people there getting things set up. Noor and Manal immediately jump in. Everyone works hard and yet the atmosphere is lighthearted and playful. And the air is filled with laughter, affection, music, and singing.

The olives are hand-picked and pulled or knocked out of each branch. The olives fall over cloths laid on the ground, then they are gathered in big buckets to be taken to the olive oil press.

Everyone is really tired now – they've been picking olives since early morning.

Then it's noon time and suddenly Manal's mom appears with a delicious home-made lunch. It's a popular Palestinian dish called maklouba, which literally means "upside down." Maklouba is made of rice, chicken, cauliflower, and different spices.

Manal's mom flips the makloubeh into a big round serving platter. The savory smell of the hot cooked meal floats through the air. Noor turns to Manal and says, "Your mom is such a great cook, I'm so hungry and can't wait to eat!"

Manal's mother calls everyone to take a break and come eat. People form a circle and sit on the ground under the olive tree and wait for the yummy food to be served. Then smiles all around as people take their first bites of makloubeh, feeling grateful for this friendly gathering, their hard work together, and this delicious food.

Right around sundown, the harvest day is finally over. Noor and Manal are exhausted and ready to go home. But they feel so content to have been part of this very special day.

Manal invites Noor to go with her the next day to visit the olive oil press, which is also owned by her dad. On Saturday morning, they both take off on a long walk to the olive press. They are carrying with them food for Manal's dad, including warm bread that Manal's mom just took out of the oven.

The olive press is a very busy place, more like a factory -- big machinery, lots of noise and activity, farmers streaming inside hauling their olives in big buckets. During the harvest season, the olive press is open day and night.

معصرة زيتون

As Manal and Noor enter, Manal's dad is already there to greet them and take them on a tour.

He starts by explaining the process of turning olives into oil, pointing to the first machine that washes the olives, then to the powerful machine that squeezes the olives and presses the oil from them.

Manal cuts open her mom's freshly baked bread and slices off two pieces.

Noor and Manal dip their bread in the golden green olive oil streaming out of the machine. "Fresh olive oil with freshly baked bread, yum-yum-yum!" Noor exclaims.

Manal says goodbye to her dad -- he'll be staying here with the olive press all night long.

Noor whispers in Manal's ear:

"Why can't your dad close the press and return in the morning?"

Manal's dad overhears and sees this as a chance to give the girls another lesson about olive oil:

"For olive oil to be of the highest quality, with a smooth taste and less acidity,"

he explains, "the olives must be pressed immediately, right after they're picked. As Palestinians our duty is to support one another like one big family. I'm committed to this work, which means I must keep the olive press open 24 hours a day, so all the farmers can have their olives pressed in time and we can ensure the high quality of our fabulous olive oil."

زيت
زيتون

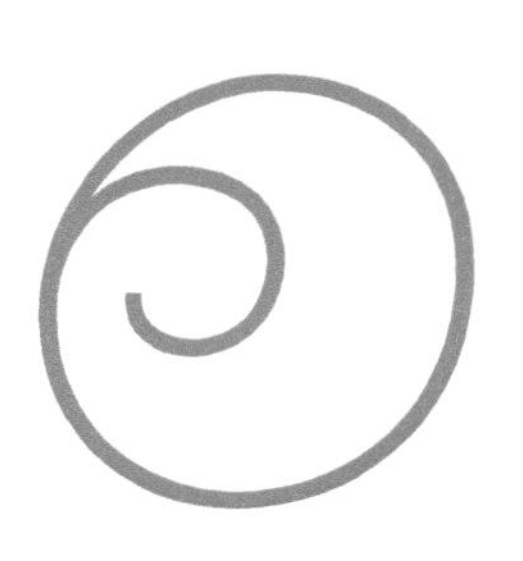

live oil is a very big deal in Palestine,"
says Manal's dad, flashing a big smile.

Noor feels so grateful to have had this awesome learning opportunity through her friend Manal and her dad.

She returns home very happy, proudly carrying a beautiful glowing bottle of olive oil freshly filled from the bottling machine.

زيتون

The End

Wafa Shami was born and raised in Ramallah, Palestine. Moved to the U.S. to pursue higher education and graduated with a Master's degree in International Studies. Since moving to the U.S. Wafa has maintained her engagement in Middle Eastern issues as a volunteer. She was inspired to write children storybooks based on her childhood after her son was born. Her first story, Easter in Ramallah, was published earlier this year. Besides being busy raising her son, who is now 5 years old, Wafa who lives in California has a passion for cooking and writes a food blog, in which she shares her family's recipes. Visit her blog at www.palestineinadish.com and follow her on social media @palestineinadish for delicious recipes.

Shaima Farouki is a Palestinian artist born in Jerusalem in 1988. A graduate of Friends School, she currently lives in Ramallah. Shaima' has a Bachelor degree from Birzeit University in Journalism and Social Sciences. She has a passion and deep interest in arts and developed her talent through practice and by attending workshops to improve her drawing skills. She has participated in many group art exhibits in Ramallah. Shaima' currently creates and sells her paintings and teaches drawing classes for beginners. She also works on illustrations for children's storybooks.

Makloubeh recipe is available on www.palestineinadish.com or visit the link:

https://palestineinadish.com/recipes/maloubeh-flipped-over-rice-cauliflower-and-chicken/